Ella
the Rose
Fairy

To Lily Grace Evans,
who will always believe in fairies

Special thanks to Sue Mongredien

ISBN-10: 0-545-07096-1
ISBN-13: 978-0-545-07096-6

12 11 10 9 8 7 6 5 4 3 2 1   9 10 11 12 13/0

Printed in the U.S.A.

First Scholastic Printing, February 2009

Ella
the Rose
Fairy

by Daisy Meadows

SCHOLASTIC INC.

New York Toronto London Auckland Sydney
Mexico City New Delhi Hong Kong Buenos Aires

The
Fairyland
Palace

Blossom
Hall

Fairy Garden

Leafley Village

Visitors' Center

I need the magic petals' powers,
To give my castle garden flowers.
I plan to use my magic well
To work against the fairies' spell.

From my wand ice magic flies,
Frosty bolts through fairy skies.
This is the crafty spell I weave
To bring the petals back to me.

Contents

Roses Need Rescuing!

"Here we are, the Chaney Court Flower Show," Mr. Walker said, looking at the steady stream of people heading toward the entrance. He smiled at his daughter, Rachel, and her best friend, Kirsty Tate. "What a flower-filled week we've had!"

"We love flowers!" Rachel said, giving Kirsty a secret smile.

"Especially since we met the Petal Fairies," Kirsty agreed in a whisper.

The girls linked arms as they followed their parents into the field where the flower show was taking place. The two families had been spending spring vacation together, and the girls had been helping the Petal Fairies find their missing magic petals. They had found six petals so far, but there was still one more to track down — the rose petal.

"What's in here?" Mr. Tate wondered aloud, as they approached a large tent.

"Ah, the rose tent," he said, reading the sign on the entrance.

Kirsty and Rachel exchanged excited glances. Maybe the missing rose petal would be inside!

A group of people were leaving the tent as the Tates and the Walkers approached.

"How disappointing," a man said gloomily. "I've never seen such unhealthy flowers!"

The Tates and the Walkers stepped inside the tent and Rachel saw that the man was right. All the roses were drooping, their petals faded and withered.

Rachel bit her lip. She and Kirsty knew exactly why the roses weren't doing well. The Petal Fairies' magic petals helped flowers grow in Fairyland and around the world. But cruel Jack Frost had sent his goblins to steal the petals. He wanted to use the petals' magic to make flowers bloom around his ice castle. When the Petal Fairies had tried to stop the goblins, the magic petals were caught in a whirl of spells and ended up in the human world! Now that the petals were missing, flowers everywhere were wilting and dying.

"Let's go and see some of the gardens instead," Mr. Walker suggested, looking sadly at the drooping roses.

Rachel turned to Kirsty as they left.
"Most of the
flowers should be
beautiful because
we've already
found the six
other petals and
sent them back to
Fairyland," she whispered.

Kirsty nodded. "But we have to rescue these roses! I bet all the dark pink flowers in the show are dying," she added.

The Petal Fairies had told the girls that each magic petal looked after its own type of flower, and other flowers of a particular color. The rose petal helped roses and all dark pink flowers grow.

"We've got to find the petal before the goblins do," Rachel whispered. "It's their

last chance to take a petal back to Jack Frost. I'm sure they'll be trying extra hard to find this one!"

The girls knew that the goblins were trying to find the fairy petals for their boss. And to make things even harder for Kirsty and Rachel, Jack Frost had given his goblins a wand full of his icy magic to use against them.

As the two families wandered down the path, Kirsty could see that the display

gardens were lined up in one long row, each in a separate area.

"What a beautiful Japanese garden!" her mom exclaimed, stopping at the first garden. "Look at that bamboo."

"And isn't the fountain pretty?" Mrs. Walker added.

Rachel couldn't concentrate on the Japanese garden, though, because she'd just spotted the sign outside the next area. It read "Fairy Garden."

She nudged Kirsty. "Look!"

The fairy garden had an
iron gate at its entrance
and was filled with
flowers in all colors
of the rainbow.
There was a
winding path
made of
glittering
stones, and a
bench perfect
for relaxing . . .
and looking for
fairies!

"Mom, can we go
into the fairy garden?"
Kirsty asked.

Mrs. Tate smiled. "Of course,"

she said. "Why don't we split
up and meet you later?
How about one hour
from now in the
refreshments tent?"
"Perfect!" Kirsty
said, as her
parents waved
good-bye and
walked on to
look at the
other gardens.
"Come on,
Rachel! The
Petal Fairies
would love it here,"
Kirsty said, pushing
open the gate and
walking in.

"Definitely," Rachel agreed, following her friend. Then, suddenly, she stopped. "Kirsty, look!"

Kirsty followed Rachel's gaze to see a large, healthy-looking rose bush covered with dark pink flowers in the back corner of the garden. "The magic petal must be near that bush." Kirsty gasped. "Otherwise, the roses wouldn't look so beautiful!"

"Yes," Rachel said happily. "So —
Uh-oh!" She broke off as she noticed that
the rose bush was rustling. "It's moving!"

Kirsty's smile vanished.
"What if the goblins
are in there?"

Luckily, there
was nobody else
in the garden,
so the girls were
able to tiptoe
down the path
and over to the
rustling roses.
Cautiously, they
peeked around the
side of the bush.

Seven horrible goblins
were pulling all the roses

off the bush! They were wearing little boys' clothes, clearly hoping to blend in with the other visitors at the show. The goblins were busy picking through the roses to find the magic petal.

"Ugh, pink!" the girls heard one goblin complain. "Such an ugly color!"

"Green is much better," another agreed.

Kirsty looked at Rachel with wide eyes, wondering how they were going to find the petal before the goblins did.

Just then, a silvery voice echoed through the air behind them. "Hello, girls! I love your pink outfits."

Kirsty and Rachel spun around to see a smiling fairy fluttering in the air!

Maze Magic

"Ella!" Kirsty cried, stepping away from
the rose bush so that she could speak
to the fairy without being overheard.

"We're so glad to see you!" Rachel
added.

Ella the Rose Fairy had long, dark,
wavy hair and wore a pink dress with a
sash around the middle.

As she opened her mouth to speak to the girls, an excited cry came from behind the rose bush.

Kirsty, Rachel, and Ella all peeked through the leaves. To their dismay, they saw that one of the goblins was holding out his hands . . . and the magic rose petal was lying in them! Rachel thought quickly. "Ella, could you use your fairy magic to make the petal float out of his hands — and over here, to us?" she suggested. "Yes!" Ella replied eagerly, pointing her wand at the bush.

A stream of sparkles swirled
from the tip of her wand and
over the thorny branches.

The girls held
their breath as they
watched the sparkles
surround the magic
petal, lift it into the
air, and carry it back
over the bush. The
plan was working!

But then a green hand
appeared and snatched the petal back.

"Oh, no you don't. You're staying with
us!" the girls heard a goblin say.

"What's going on?" another asked.
Then three goblin faces appeared around
the side of the bush.

"We should have guessed," sneered
one. "It's those silly girls with a silly fairy."

"Searching for the petal, are you?"
another gloated. "Too bad!"

"May I please have it?" Ella asked
sweetly. "It *is* mine, you know!"

"Not anymore, it isn't!" The goblin
holding the petal laughed. "It's ours. And
we're bringing it to Jack Frost. He'll be
very happy with us!"

Just then, one of the
goblins burst out
laughing, pointing
at the girls and
Ella. "Look at
them, all wearing
yucky pink!"
he cackled.

"Pink stinks!" another yelled. "We're out of here!"

And with that, the goblins rushed out of the back of the fairy garden, taking the rose petal with them.

"Follow them!" Kirsty cried.

Ella swooped down to hide under Rachel's hair as the girls raced after the goblins. The goblins ran past an English cottage garden, then a rock garden, before turning into a maze of hedges.

Kirsty had just enough time to glimpse the sign as she ran by. It read, *Chaney Court Hedge Maze. Can you find the statue in the middle?*

The goblins scattered,
each charging down
different paths.

"Which one has
the petal?" Rachel
cried, not sure
which goblin
to chase.

"I'll turn you
both into
fairies," Ella
decided. "Then
we can fly and
hopefully spot the
petal from above!"

In a shower of pink
sparkles, Kirsty and
Rachel found themselves
shrinking to fairy-size.

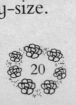

Gorgeous, glittery
wings appeared on
their backs, and they
immediately
zoomed up above
the maze.
"I can see three
goblins," Kirsty
said, pointing
them out. "Oh,
and there's
another. . . ."
"There's one in
the middle, by
the statue,"
Rachel added.
"And look at what
he's holding!"
"My petal!" Ella cried joyfully.

The three friends zipped toward the statue. "Ella, if you turn us back to our normal size, Rachel and I can try to get your petal back from him," Kirsty suggested.

Ella lifted her wand, but Rachel stopped her.

"Hold on," she said, pointing down at the maze. "The other goblins are almost at the center, too. I don't think we'll be able to get the petal away from all of them."

Ella nodded. "Let me make the maze a little bit more difficult for them," she said with a sly grin.

She flitted over and sprinkled some fairy dust along the path that led to the center of the maze. Instantly, a new section of hedge started to grow, blocking the entrance to the clearing where the statue stood.

The goblin who was already standing by the statue stared at the new hedge. "Hey! I'm trapped!" he yelled.

"And his friends won't be able to come to his rescue!" Kirsty realized with a giggle. "Super smart, Ella!"

Rachel grinned. "Now let's get that petal!" she cried.

Pink Lightning

Rachel and Kirsty swooped down to the
center of the maze. Once they landed,
Ella turned them back into girls with
another wave of her wand.

The goblin was surprised to see them
appear in front of him. "Help! Those girls
have found me!" he shouted in alarm.

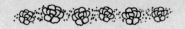

Kirsty grinned. "You can shout as much as you want, but they won't be able to help you."

Rachel held out her hand. "You might as well give us the petal now," she told him, "because you're trapped in here with us!"

The goblin hid the petal behind his back. "I'm not giving it to you," he said stubbornly.

"Hang on! We're coming!" another goblin's voice called from somewhere over the hedge.

"It's no use," the goblin with the petal shouted back. "I'm stuck in here with their pesky fairy magic!"

"Well, those fairies should know by now that we have our own magic!" came another shout. The girls jumped and looked around, because the voice sounded very close behind them.

There was a rustling noise, and Rachel and Kirsty turned to see a wand poking through the hedge — a wand held by a goblin's green hand!

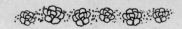

Before the girls could do or say
anything, one of the goblins started
chanting a spell.

"This will stop those girls, I think.
Lightning bolts, zap all things pink!" he
cried from the other side of the hedge.

Kirsty looked down at her top in
horror. She was wearing pink — and so
were Rachel and Ella.

They were all
about to get
blasted by the
goblins' icy magic!
"Hide!" yelled
Kirsty, ducking behind
the statue. The next
instant, lightning bolts
fizzed through the
hedge right at her.

CRASH! One bolt hit the statue — and to the girls' surprise, it turned the statue bright pink!

CRASH! Another bolt struck the goblin with the petal.

Rachel and Kirsty stared at him in shock. He had turned pink, right before their eyes!

Ella gave a tinkling laugh. "It's because of the way the goblin said the spell," she explained. "When he said 'Lightning bolts, zap all things pink', he wanted for lightning to strike everything that's pink—but instead, it's *turning* things pink!"

The goblin with the petal didn't seem to notice his color change. "It didn't work!" he shouted through the hedge. "The lightning missed that pesky pink fairy and her friends!"

Three goblins peered through the hedge — and immediately burst into laughter. "Hey, pink looks good on you!" one of them teased.

"What?" demanded the goblin with

the petal. He looked down at
himself and gasped. "I'm pink!" he
wailed.

"It's definitely your color." Rachel
giggled.

"Very flattering," Ella agreed,
sputtering with laughter.

"It's not funny!" the pink goblin
snapped, stomping his foot. "Turn me
green again right now!"

Once the goblins on the other side of the hedge had managed to stop laughing, the wand poked through the branches again. The girls heard another goblin clear his throat, to cast a second spell.

"Oh, no you don't!" Kirsty cried, darting forward and snatching the wand right out of his hand.

"Hey!" came a surprised shout. "Give that back!"

"No way," Kirsty replied happily. But she then gulped in alarm, because the magic hedge plants that Ella had conjured up suddenly vanished in a burst of pink sparkles. And, all at once, the other goblins charged into the middle of the maze!

A Frosty
Atmosphere

Ella quickly turned the girls back into
fairies, so they could zoom up into the air
and escape the goblins. The goblins'
wand in Kirsty's hand became fairy-
sized, too.

"Hey — give our wand back!" one of
the goblins shouted.

"Jack Frost will be mad if we come back without it," another said, worried. He jumped up, trying to catch the girls.

"Sorry, guys!" Rachel grinned. "But —"

She broke off as she spotted a girl in a lilac T-shirt walking close to the center of the maze.

"Oh no!" Rachel gulped. "Look!"

"We can't let her see the goblins!" Ella cried.

Kirsty's mind raced, until she remembered she had a magic wand in her hand. She quickly pointed it down at the goblins and tried to think up a spell. "Whisk this magic far away,

back to Jack Frost's hideaway!" she
declared.

A magical wind began to blow around
the goblins, sweeping them up into the
air. But then Kirsty felt a cold wind
tugging at her, too.

"Oh no!" Ella exclaimed.
"We're part of the magic,
too. We're caught up in
the spell!"

Kirsty gulped as the
wind grew even
stronger. "You
mean . . ." she began.

Ella nodded. "We're on
our way to Jack Frost!"

Everything blurred before the
girls' eyes as they were whisked up in the
magical whirlwind with the goblins.

When the whirl of magic
finally died away, the girls
and Ella saw that they
were hovering in
midair, a short
distance from
Jack Frost's ice
castle. Below
them, the
goblins were
lying in the
snow, a heap
of tangled
arms and legs.

Jack Frost turned
in surprise, from
where he'd been feeding
his snow geese at the pond.

"Oh, it's you!" he snapped at the goblins. "What do you have for me?" Kirsty, Rachel, and Ella quickly fluttered behind a nearby tree, hoping Jack Frost wouldn't notice them. Luckily, his eye was drawn straight to the goblin at the bottom of the heap, who was still bright pink. "What on Earth . . .?" Jack Frost

sputtered. "What have you been doing?"

"It wasn't my fault!" the pink goblin moaned. "Besides, look what I brought for you!" he added proudly, wiggling his hand out from under the other goblins. He was still clutching the rose petal between his fingers.

"At last! A magic petal of my own!" Jack Frost cried triumphantly. "Now I will have all the flowers I want growing around my castle!"

Poor Ella could hardly watch. "If Jack Frost gets his hands on my petal, I might never see it again," she whispered miserably.

"What if Kirsty and I distract him?" Rachel suggested. "Then you can fly over and grab the petal while he's not looking!"

"OK!" Ella said, her face brightening. "Let's try it."

As Ella headed toward the petal, the girls flew out into the open, behind Jack Frost.

Kirsty saw that Jack Frost was just reaching out to grab the petal.

"Hey, Jack Frost!" she called quickly.
"Aren't you wondering where your
wand is?"

Jack Frost turned in surprise, and glared
when he saw Kirsty and Rachel.

"We've got it!" Rachel added.

"And we're going to cast a spell on
you!" Kirsty cried.

"How did you get my wand?" Jack
Frost bellowed furiously.

He immediately marched away from

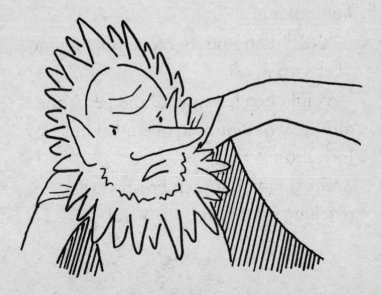

the goblins, toward the girls. "I'll take that, thank you," he snapped. He stared hard at the wand, then lifted his hand and muttered a magic word. Instantly, the wand flew from Kirsty's grasp back to its master.

With a horrible grin, Jack Frost pointed the wand at the girls. "Maybe this will teach you to stop causing trouble!" he told them. And then, as he whispered a spell, a freezing lightning bolt came shooting out of the wand — straight toward Rachel and Kirsty.

Frozen Flowers

"Hide!" shouted Rachel. Quickly, she
and Kirsty hid behind the tree trunk.
Neither of them could see Ella now, but
they both really hoped she'd been able to
grab her petal.

Kirsty peeked around the tree to look
for Ella, and then pulled back in alarm as

two more lightning bolts flashed past. She
and Rachel clung to each other.

"What are we going
to do?" Kirsty asked
as lightning bolts
whistled past
the tree, barely
missing the girls.
"I don't know,"
Rachel replied.
"Sooner or later,
one of these is going to hit us!"
But as the girls looked at each other in
panic, Kirsty saw a stream of pink fairy
dust sparkling in the sky above them. As
she watched, the fairy dust began to turn
into brightly colored flowers that rained
down to the ground between the girls
and Jack Frost. More and more of them

appeared in the sky and floated down,
creating a curtain of falling flowers.
And when Jack Frost's lightning bolts
hit the bright blooms, they bounced
right off.

"The flowers are acting like a shield,"
Kirsty realized.

"It must be petal magic!" Rachel cried in delight.

"And, look, there are the Petal Fairies!" Kirsty exclaimed, pointing to where Ella was flitting in the air, along with the other Petal Fairies: Tia, Pippa, Louise, Charlotte, Olivia, and Danielle. They were all smiling and waving at Kirsty and Rachel.

"Ella must have rescued her petal when we distracted Jack Frost." Rachel laughed. "And now all of the Petal Fairies have come to rescue us!"

Kirsty nodded happily. "Look!" she said, pointing to the curtain of flowers. "When the icy lightning bolts hit the magic wall, they freeze the falling flowers. Aren't they pretty?"

Rachel grinned. "Yes. And, look —
Jack Frost obviously thinks so, too!" She
pointed to Jack Frost, who was no longer
hurling lightning bolts at the girls.
Instead, he was bending down and
scooping up armfuls of the frozen flowers.

"Hey, you guys!" he shouted to his
goblins. "Come and help me gather all of
these. They're perfect for decorating my
castle gardens!"

The goblins,
who'd untangled
themselves by now,
ran over to help.
"Look at these
frozen sunflowers!"
one of them exclaimed.
"They'll look good over here," he added,
planting them in the ground. Being
frozen, they stood up straight and
sparkled brilliantly with frost.

"These tulips are
nice," another goblin
sighed. "I think I'll
take a bunch home
to my mom."

Ella and the other
Petal Fairies flew down
to join the girls.

"Thank you for saving us from Jack Frost," Kirsty said.

Ella laughed. "We're the ones who should be thanking you," she told the girls. "You did a great job — again!"

Tia smiled. "Let's leave Jack Frost to his frozen flowers," she suggested, taking Kirsty by the hand.

Louise came over and took Rachel's hand. "Yes, let's go," she said.

"Where to?" Kirsty asked, feeling excited.

Olivia smiled. "To the Fairyland palace, of course!" she said. "King Oberon and Queen Titania are waiting to see you!"

A New Friend

The seven Petal Fairies led Kirsty and
Rachel away from Jack Frost's castle
to the beautiful gardens outside the
Fairyland palace. There, the girls saw the
fairy king and queen waiting for them.
They were standing next to a pool that
glittered in the sunlight.

"Good job!" Queen Titania said

warmly as the girls landed. "We
watched everything
right here, in the
seeing pool.
Rachel and
Kirsty, you
have done a
fantastic job
helping the
fairies get all seven
of their magic petals back."

"Yes, we couldn't have done it without
them," Charlotte the Sunflower Fairy
said, beaming.

"And now that Jack Frost has his
everlasting ice flowers, he won't bother
our Petal Fairies again," the king added.
He shook his head, looking frustrated. "If
he had just come and asked us for help in

the first place, none of this would have happened. He didn't need to steal the petals."

"Yes!" Queen Titania said. "We certainly understand that flowers are meant to be shared. I'm glad Jack Frost is happy with his palace garden now."

Then Ella waved her wand over Kirsty and Rachel and, to their surprise, garlands of rainbow-colored flowers appeared around their necks.

"Thank you!" Rachel exclaimed.
"They're beautiful!"

"Of course," Ella replied. "They're just
a little something to
remember the Petal
Fairies by."
The queen lifted her
wand. "I'm afraid
it's time for you to
return to the human
world now," she said.
"Oh, yes, we're supposed
to be meeting our parents soon," Kirsty
agreed.

"Good-bye, girls," Ella said, giving
Rachel and Kirsty a last hug. "And
thanks again!"

"Good-bye," the two girls chorused.
The queen waved her wand over them,

and they were whisked away from Fairyland in a blur of color. Seconds later, they found themselves back in the maze, and at their normal size.

"It's strange being here without Ella or the goblins," Kirsty said, looking around.

Rachel nodded. "It's so much more quiet!" She laughed.

"And look," Kirsty said, "our flower garlands have turned into necklaces. Aren't they pretty?"

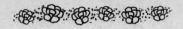

Rachel saw that Kirsty was right —
they were both wearing necklaces made
of glittering, flower-shaped beads. There
were seven different beads that matched
the colors of the magic petals. The
necklaces were almost as beautiful as the
real flowers!

Just then, a girl with a lilac T-shirt
walked into the center of the maze.

Of course! Kirsty thought. *It's the girl who was about to reach the middle when we were whisked away to Fairyland.*

"Hi," said the girl. "My name's Arabella Diers. This maze is hard, isn't it? It's taken me forever to get here!"

"I'm Rachel," Rachel replied. She didn't know what to say about the maze. After all, she and Kirsty had flown to the middle. They hadn't actually had to find their way through the maze at all. Suddenly, she realized that they didn't have a clue how to get out!

"It is hard," Kirsty was saying. "In fact, we can't remember the way out. Can you?"

Arabella nodded. "I think so," she said.
"Follow me!" As she turned to lead the
way out, she caught sight of the girls'
necklaces. "Ooh! They're pretty," she
commented.

It didn't take the three girls long to find
the start of the maze.

"Here we are!" Arabella said proudly
as they reached the exit.

"Thank you," Kirsty said. Impulsively,
she pulled off her fairy necklace and

handed it to
Arabella.
"Here — have
this," she said.
"To say thanks
for helping us."
Arabella's
face lit up.

"Oh, thank you!" she breathed, looking starry-eyed with delight. Rachel and Kirsty grinned.

"That was nice of you," Rachel said, taking her own necklace off as Arabella walked away. "If you like, we could try and make my necklace into anklets. Then we can each have one."

Suddenly, she gasped as the necklace started to shimmer with a sparkly pink light. As the girls watched, the necklace split apart and transformed itself into two pretty anklets.

Kirsty stared at Rachel, her mouth wide open. "How did you do that?" she gasped.

Rachel was just as surprised as Kirsty. "I didn't do anything! The fairies must have been watching over us," she said with a smile. "Thank you, Petal Fairies!" She handed an anklet to Kirsty, and both girls fastened them around their ankles.

"We'd better go and meet our parents," Rachel said. "Come on!"

The girls rushed over to the refreshments tent, just in time to see their parents sitting down by a beautiful, flowering rose bush. "Aren't these fantastic?" Mrs. Walker said to Rachel and Kirsty, sniffing one of the blooms.

"Yes, and you wouldn't believe it, but when we passed the rose tent a minute ago, all the roses were looking much better!" Mr. Tate put in.

The girls exchanged happy glances.

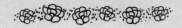

Now that the rose petal was back in Fairyland, it was working its special magic all over the world again. Roses and dark pink flowers everywhere would be growing beautifully!

Mr. Walker smiled at the girls. "Did you have fun?" he asked.

"Yes, thanks," Rachel told him. "The maze was really good."

"Yes, it was a lot of fun!" Kirsty added.
The two girls grinned at one another.
They both loved their fairy adventures.
Being friends with the fairies made
everything fun!

THE Dance FAIRIES

Rachel and Kirsty helped all
seven Petal Fairies, but now there's
more trouble in Fairyland.
The Dance Fairies need their help!

Join the adventure in this
special sneak peek of

Bethany
the Ballet Fairy!

Fairies in a Whirl

"I'm really excited about this!" exclaimed Rachel Walker, smiling at her best friend, Kirsty Tate. "I *love* ballet."

"Me, too," Kirsty agreed, raising her voice above the noise of the train as it rattled over the bumpy tracks. "I've never seen *Swan Lake* before."

"I've heard that this is a great

production," Kirsty's mom said. "The scenery is supposed to be beautiful."

"Well, let's hope it keeps Dad awake!" Kirsty laughed, glancing at her dad. He was fast asleep in the corner seat of the train. "I'm so glad you could come, Rachel. Wasn't it lucky that your school got out for vacation the day before ours did? You wouldn't have been here in time to come with us, otherwise."

Rachel nodded. Because their families lived far apart, she was staying with Kirsty for the whole week of the school vacation.

"We'll be in the city soon," said Mrs. Tate, as the train pulled into a station. "This is the last stop before we get there."

Kirsty stared out the window as the train slowed. Suddenly, her attention was caught by a flash of icy blue streaking past. Curious, Kirsty leaned forward for a closer look.

To her amazement, she saw seven little fairies tumbling through the air on a tiny icy whirlwind! As Kirsty watched, the fairies landed safely in one of the baskets of flowers suspended from the station roof.

Kirsty and Rachel knew a lot about fairies because the two girls shared an amazing secret. They were best friends with the fairies! They often helped them to defeat Jack Frost and his nasty goblins, who were always causing trouble. Now it looked like their fairy friends might need the girls' help again!

There's magic in every book

The Rainbow Fairies
Books #1-7

The Weather Fairies
Books #1-7

The Jewel Fairies
Books #1-7

The Pet Fairies
Books #1-7

The Fun Day Fairies
Books #1-7

SCHOLASTIC

www.scholastic.com
www.rainbowmagiconline.com

HIT entertainment

FAI